P9-BBV-491
This book belongs to:

All the Best Things About
Being in a Wedding

Illustrated by
Linda Hill Griffith

Cover and internal design by Krista Joy Johnson/Sourebooks

Published by Sourcebooks, Inc.
P.O. Box 4410, Naperville, Illinois 60567-4410
(630) 961-3900
Fax: (630) 961-2168
www.sourcebooks.com

Source of Production: 1010 Printing, China
Date of Production: December 2021
Run Number: 5024599

Printed and bound in China.
OGP 30

To My
Most Special
Flower Girl

____

____

____

Today is a very special day for Sophie. Auntie Sarah and her boyfriend Andrew have come for dinner.

"We have a surprise for you, Sophie," said Auntie Sarah after dessert.

Sophie smiled. She loved surprises!

"Andrew and I are getting married, and we want you to be the flower girl at our wedding!"

"Hooray!" Sophie shouted. "Can I, Mommy? Please?"

"Sure," Mommy said. "Do you know what being a flower girl means, Sophie?"

"Hmmm..." Sophie wondered. She wasn't really sure. When Sophie's friend Emma was a flower girl, she held her little brother's hand and they walked down the aisle together. Her friend Abigail held a big ball of flower petals called a pomander. Her cousin Madison even rode down the aisle in a wagon!

"Being a flower girl is very important," Auntie Sarah explained. "You'll be my special helper on our wedding day. You'll get to wear a beautiful dress and walk down the aisle during the ceremony. It's like being a princess for the day!"

Sophie was so excited to shop for her dress. There were so many pretty ones to choose from! Some were big and poufy, and others were soft and silky.

"How about this one, Sophie?" Auntie Sarah asked.

Sophie tried it on and twirled around and around. Perfect!

Sophie also got sparkly white shoes with a pretty buckle shaped like a flower.

Every day, Sophie looked at her beautiful outfit hanging in the closet. She could hardly wait for the chance to wear it.

Sophie still had a lot of questions.

"What will I do the day of the wedding, Mommy?"

"You will carry a pretty basket full of flower petals, and your job will be to scatter them down the aisle right before Auntie Sarah comes out."

The night before the wedding, everybody got together to practice walking down the aisle.

"Try not to walk too quickly or too slowly," Mommy explained. "And be sure to smile!"

Later, Auntie Sarah told Sophie about a special tradition.

"Sometimes, for good luck, brides like to wear something old, something new, something borrowed, and something blue," Auntie Sarah said. "For something old, I'm going to carry my grandmother's beautiful handkerchief."

Andrew's nephew David was there too. David was going to be the ring bearer, another big job.

"You and David must remember to always be polite and patient and calm during the wedding," Mommy said.

"I know, Mommy," Sophie said. "I'll be super-duper good!"

"And I'll be good too," said David. "No yelling, no screaming, and no playing in the mud!

"Wake up, Sophie—today is the day!"

After a big healthy breakfast, Mommy curled Sophie's hair and tied it back with some pretty purple ribbons to match her dress.

It took awhile to get ready, but when she finally looked in the mirror, Sophie looked like a real princess!

Before the wedding started, Sophie, Auntie Sarah, and the bridesmaids posed for pictures.

Sophie spotted a piece of pretty lace caught in the lilacs, but before she could grab it, she heard Auntie Sarah say, "Come along, ladies! It's time to walk down the aisle!"

As they walked into the church, Auntie Sarah said, "Wait! My handkerchief is gone! I must have lost it!"

Sophie was very worried. But then she had an idea…

"I'll be right back," she told them. "Don't start without me!"

Sophie ran to the garden as fast as her new shoes could carry her. She picked up the lace handkerchief in the lilacs.

Then she ran back to Auntie Sarah.

"Oh!" Auntie Sarah gasped when she saw Sophie. "You found it!"

"You saved the day!" Mommy said, and hugged her. "Now we're ready to walk down the aisle at last."

Sophie was a little nervous, but she knew she could do it. When it was her turn, she took a deep breath and began to walk down the aisle, just like she'd practiced.

When she was done, she sat down next to Mommy to watch the ceremony.

Now that all the hard work was done, it was time to have the wedding reception—a big party where everyone celebrates!

Auntie Sarah and Uncle Andrew joined all the guests in a big room with lots of tables and had a special dance together.

"Sophie, you were so wonderful today—you saved the wedding with your quick thinking! I am so proud of you, and I love you so much. Thank you for being the most special flower girl a bride could have."